Sharing Grandma's Gift

Shelley Berlin Parrish

Illustrated by Kristi Petosa-Sigel

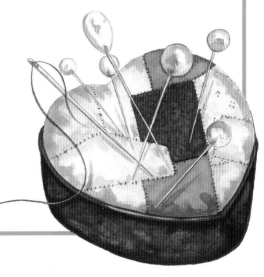

Sharing Grandma's Gift

Illustrations by Kristi Petosa-Sigel
Cover and Text Design by Susan Picatti

04 03 02 01 00   5 4 3 2 1

ISBN 0-89716-936-0
Library of Congress Catalog Card Number: 99-64040

First Printing February 2000

Published by Peanut Butter Publishing
Milwaukee, Wisconsin
Printed in Korea

Peanut Butter Publishing
5630 N. Lake Drive • Milwaukee, Wisconsin 53217
414-906-0600 • e-mail: pbpub@execpc.com
Milwaukee • Seattle • Vancouver BC • Los Angeles • Portland • Denver

For all who have shared a special gift...

I will always be with you...

SBP

Allie loved to watch the women in her family do their stitching. She would sit next to Grandma, content to watch Grandma's fingers work the floss into the tiny holes of the needle-point canvas. Her brown eyes grew big at the sight of the silky, rainbow-colored floss.

One day, without looking up from her needlepoint, Grandma said, "Allie, you have a wonderful collection of colored floss. By chance do you have any room in it for this color?"

"Do I have any room?" Allie thought. She knew exactly where the new color would fit in! "Grandma, I love that color! How did you know?"

Grandma smiled and kept on stitching. She just knew, the way Grandmas always do.

Allie also liked to sit next to her mom, watching her mom's long fingers patiently stitch her handsewn quilts. Together, they hunted through the scrap box, looking for just the right odds and ends of fabric pieces for the quilt.

"Ooh, look at this piece!" Allie thought to herself as she gazed at the colorful fabric. Already she had plans to save it for the first quilt she would make one day. Allie never needed to ask her mom for the cloth. Her mom always gave Allie the piece. She just knew, the way mothers always do.

Meanwhile, the patches of her mom's Sampler Quilt fit together like the pieces of a jigsaw puzzle.

Each square was different, with its own pattern and colors. When the quilt was finished, Allie's mom hung it on the wall.

People who came over to visit exclaimed, "What a beautiful quilt! Please tell us its story."

Allie's mom explained, "My quilts are made with love. They will stay safe and protected on the walls for a very long time. Someday, each of my three children will have a quilt to remember me by." She added, "Allie, the Wedding Ring Quilt will be yours one day."

"Can I have the quilt *now*?" Allie asked.

"No, you'll have to wait until the time is right," her mom answered. "For now, will you keep its story?"

Allie was puzzled. What story did the Wedding Ring Quilt have to tell? Still, she nodded solemnly and answered, "Yes, I will keep its story."

One day, Grandma, Allie, and her mom sat together, stitching and talking all the while. Grandma admired the quilt that her daughter was working on and asked Allie's mom, "When will *you* make a quilt for *me*?"

Allie's mom promised, "When I have time, I'll make one for you, Mother." Allie wondered when that might be.

The next spring, Allie's mom was working on the Bear Paw Quilt for Allie's brother when Grandma became very sick.

The doctors said that she did not have long to live. While her eyes welled up with tears, Allie cried, "Mom, it's not fair! What will Papa do without her?"

Holding Allie tight in her arms, her mom replied, "What will *all* of us do without her?"

For the next two months, Allie and her mom spent afternoons talking and stitching by Grandma's bedside.

Allie looked forward to these special times with Grandma and her mom. She watched as her mom's fingers skipped quickly across the unfinished quilt. The tiny stitches joined each bear paw together just so.

As the hours passed, Allie's mom told wonderful stories of when she was a little girl in Grandma's house. It was fun to listen to all of the stories unfold.

Allie could picture Grandma as a young mother, teaching her daughter how to sew.

Allie especially loved to hear her mother talk about sundown on Friday evenings. "Like generations of Jewish women before us, Grandma and I would light the *Shabbat* candles together. As we gazed into the gentle flames, all the world seemed right," said her mom.

Allie thought that from now on, each *Shabbat* when she and her mother lit the candles together, Grandma would be in their prayers.

After returning home from a visit with Grandma, Allie's mom took Allie into the bedroom to look at the Wedding Ring Quilt hanging on the wall. Her mom wondered aloud just how many hours she had spent handstitching each ring of that quilt.

Looking down at Allie, she explained, "In olden times, a mother gave a quilt, just like this one, to her daughter as a wedding present. Like the gold wedding band, each ring of the quilt symbolizes the circle of life, no beginning or end, forever. While beautiful to look at, the quilts were used to warm and comfort the young family in their new home. Through the years, each quilt gathered a special story to pass on."

Allie's mom turned and smiled, "When you become a young bride ready to stand under the wedding *chupah*, this quilt will be my gift to you."

Allie imagined herself in another place and time. Deep in thought, she pictured herself as a young bride under the wedding canopy, dressed in a sparkling white gown of satin and lace.

She imagined her mother giving her the gift of the quilt at last.

Looking up at her mom, Allie asked, "If my Wedding Ring Quilt just hangs on the wall, what story will it have to tell?"

Allie's mom, deep in her own thoughts, was imagining another bride from years past. She gazed upon an old, worn wedding photograph, brown from age. The photograph had been taken nearly fifty years ago.

The young couple under the *chupah* were her own parents, Allie's Grandma and Papa.

Turning her thoughts back to her daughter, Allie's mom sighed and said, "In just one month it will be Grandma and Papa's Golden Wedding Anniversary."

Allie thought long and hard. Fifty years seemed like a very long time to share with another person.

"My Wedding Ring Quilt looks beautiful on the wall, but still, I wish it had a story to tell," she thought.

A moment later, a sparkle came to her big brown eyes. "I know!" she exclaimed. "I have the perfect present for Grandma and Papa's Golden Anniversary! Remember how Grandma wished for one of your handsewn quilts? Can we give *my* quilt to Grandma? Oh, please, Mom?"

Together, Allie and her mom gently lifted the Wedding Ring Quilt off the wall. When they noticed a tear on the back, they understood that even the wall had not been able to keep the quilt safe.

"It's perfect, even with the tear!" Allie said excitedly.

Later that day, Allie laid the quilt on Grandma's lap. Happy tears came to Grandma's eyes as she smiled at Allie's gift. The quilt had looked beautiful covering the wall, but Allie thought it looked even more beautiful covering Grandma.

Each day, while her body grew weaker, Grandma's spirit grew stronger. The story of the quilt was coming alive.

Everyone who came to see Grandma resting under the quilt exclaimed, "What a beautiful quilt! Please tell us its story."

Allie would proudly answer, "This is the quilt my mom made for me! It's a Wedding Ring Quilt. Each ring is like a gold wedding band. It shows how life is like a circle that goes on forever. Since Grandma always wanted one of my mom's handsewn quilts, I gave her this one. It's my gift for her and Papa's Golden Wedding Anniversary." Secretly, Allie wondered if Grandma would live to see their special day. She counted the days while Grandma breathed slowly and peacefully.

One quiet, sunny day, Grandma took Allie's hand in her own and said, "One day soon, you will not be able to see me anymore, but as long as you remember special times we had together, I will always be with you. You will be able to feel me watching over you. I will help you over all the bad times and celebrate all of the good times with you. Show me every day how wonderful you are, and I will have peace and joy. I love you very much." Allie gently squeezed Grandma's hand in her own.

Grandma took her last breath just four days before the special day. Allie felt her heart break when it came time to say goodbye and take back the Wedding Ring Quilt.

At the funeral, Rabbi Shapiro reminded Allie's family of the richness of Grandma's life. He explained, "It is like an elegant and colorful cloak surrounding her soul. Through this embracing garment, her children will continue to feel the protectiveness of her arms around them.

"It is a special gift that will continue to warm and strengthen them forevermore."

Allie and her mom looked at each other through teary eyes, understanding. Allie felt comforted knowing that Grandma had died snuggled in the quilt that her mom had made for her.

She would always remember the beauty that Grandma had brought to the Wedding Ring Quilt. Just like the rings of the quilt, Grandma's love was never-ending. Allie knew it would go on forever in their hearts.

Slowly, a gentle smile came to her lips and her eyes shone brightly. "Mom!" she whispered. "Can it be? Now my quilt has a story! By sharing my quilt with Grandma, I gave it a story to pass on to *my* children and grand-children!"

Smiling proudly at Allie, her mom answered, "Yes, you certainly have."

After the funeral, family and friends gathered to observe *Shiva*. There were seven days and nights of prayer and mourning. On Grandma and Papa's anniversary, everyone joined together like the rings of the quilt to share stories of Grandma.

There was laughter and there were tears. Like the tiny stitches that bind a quilt, precious memories of Grandma would keep her bound in their hearts forever.

Grandma's house was filled with love. Allie had a strange and wonderful feeling that Grandma was there with them. She just knew, the way you sometimes do.

Now Allie and her mom sit side by side as they continue their stitching journeys. Her mom lovingly stitches a crib quilt for Allie's baby cousin who has just been born. The new baby girl was named after Allie's grandma.

Carefully, Allie pieces together her very first Patchwork Quilt using the scraps of fabric her mom had given her. She thoughtfully fingers the silky rainbow-colored floss she had collected from Grandma. Patiently she ties the knots that will hold her quilt together.

Already, Allie imagines herself snuggled inside her Patchwork Quilt, as a new story begins to unfold.

GLOSSARY

Floss   A thick type of thread used for needlework and craft projects.

Needlepoint   A craft that uses needles, floss, and a canvas with tiny holes to create decorations, including items such as pictures and pillow covers.

Renoir   Pierre-Auguste Renoir was an artist who was born in France in 1841. Renoir liked to paint colorful flowers, beautiful women, and happy children. He died in 1919 at the age of 78.

Quilts   Quilts are warm blankets made by sewing together two layers of fabric with padding in between. Quilts come in many different patterns and colors, which make each one unique. Some quilts are hundreds of years old and were sewn by hand. Quilts today can be sewn by hand or with a sewing machine.

Shabbat   *Shabbat* is the seventh day of the Jewish week. It begins Friday at sundown and ends Saturday at sundown. *Shabbat* is a time set aside to rest, study, pray, and be with family.

Chupah   At a Jewish wedding, the bride and groom stand under a canopy called a *chupah*. Usually held up by four poles, the *chupah* can be made of cloth or covered in flowers.

Rabbi   *Rabbi* means "teacher." Rabbis help people learn Jewish laws and customs and lead them in prayers. Rabbis also participate in life-cycle events such as birth, marriage, and death.

Shiva   After a Jewish funeral, family and friends gather at the home of the closest relative of the person who has died. During these visits, people share stories and special memories. People "sit *Shiva*" for seven days. *Shiva* is the Hebrew word for "seven" and refers to these seven days of mourning.